The War

Anaïs Vaugelade

CAROLRHODA BOOKS, INC./MINNEAPOLIS

THE REDS AND THE BLUES were at war.
Each morning, the soldiers walked to the battlefield.
Each evening, the survivors brought home
the wounded and the dead.

The war had lasted for so long that no one
could remember why it had begun.

VICTOR THE SECOND, king of the Reds, counted his soldiers and counted them again. "Ten plus twenty is thirty. Add another fifty, and that makes eighty. Only eighty soldiers! That's not enough soldiers to win the war." And he began to cry.

But happily for him, Victor the Second, king of the Reds, had a son named Julius. When he saw his father begin to lose hope, Julius called, "Have courage, Papa!" And the king felt his courage rise.

ARMAND THE TWELFTH, who ruled the Blues, also had eighty soldiers and a son. But when Armand the Twelfth worried, his son had nothing to say.

ARMAND THE TWELFTH'S son was named Fabien,
and he wasn't very interested in war. Actually,
Fabien wasn't interested in much of anything.
He spent his days in the park, sitting in a tree.
One day, Prince Fabien received a letter from Prince Julius.
It read:

Our fathers are nearly out of soldiers.
If you are brave enough, prepare your horse and armor
and meet me on the battlefield tomorrow morning.
We will duel, and the winner of the duel will win the war for
his kingdom.

Sincerely,
Julius

Fabien sighed.
He didn't like horses very much.

THE PRINCES MET on the battlefield early the next morning.
Julius rode in on a warhorse. Fabien sat on the back of a sheep.
"En garde!" cried Julius, to start the duel.
"Baa!" bleated the sheep.
Julius's frightened horse reared straight up.

JULIUS FELL to the ground.

"Are you hurt?" asked Fabien.

But Julius was more than hurt. The fall had killed him.

The Red soldiers screamed, "You cheated! The duel was a trick!"

Fabien wanted to explain that it was an accident.

But the soldiers had lances and spears, so he decided to run away.

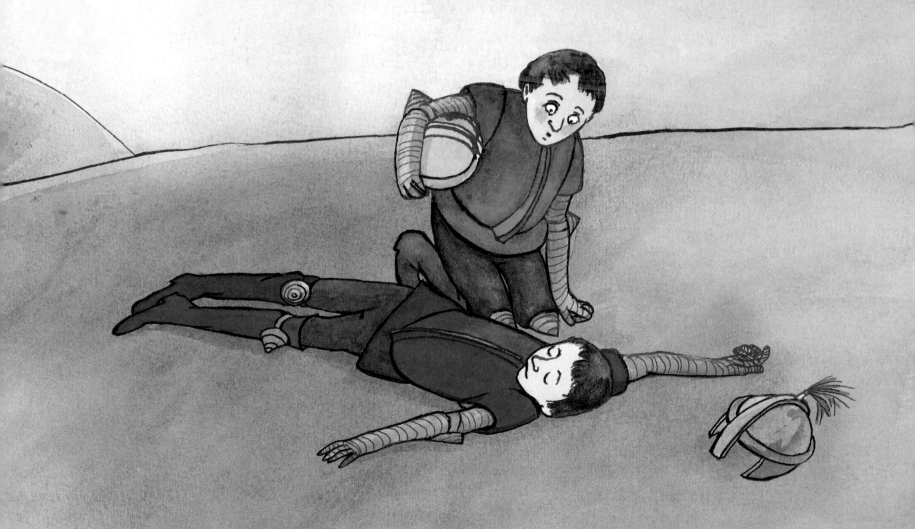

ARMAND THE TWELFTH, king of the Blues, was waiting for his son.
"You should be ashamed," he scolded Fabien.
"But I did nothing," Fabien protested.
"Precisely. At least Prince Julius tried to win the war," growled his father.
"Shame and double shame! I banish you from my kingdom!"

PRINCE FABIEN HID in the park.
As morning turned to afternoon,
the soldiers returned to the battlefield,
and Fabien had an idea.
He wrote two letters—one for Armand the
Twelfth, king of the Blues, and the other
for Victor the Second, king of the Reds.

THE TWO LETTERS said exactly the same thing.

I am with Basil the Fourth, king of the Yellows.
He has given me a huge army.
If you are brave enough,
prepare your horses and your armor!
I will meet you on the battlefield tomorrow.

Sincerely,
Fabien

Armand the Twelfth read his letter that evening.
"My good-for-nothing son with an army?" he roared.
"He'll have eight soldiers, at the most.
I'll grind them into sausage!"

When Victor the Second read his letter, he shrugged his
shoulders. He would crush Prince Fabien for having
cheated in the duel with Prince Julius.
He put the letter in his pocket and went to bed.

EACH ARMY APPROACHED the battlefield the next morning.
When he saw the Blue Army marching toward him, the king of the
Reds spluttered: "What are *you* doing here? Leave this battlefield!"
"We're here to face the Yellow Army," explained the king of the Blues.
"I don't understand," complained the king of the Reds.

The kings compared their letters and found they were identical.
"How many soldiers do you suppose he'll have?" wondered Armand the Twelfth.
"Perhaps eight, or eighty, or eight hundred," guessed Victor the Second.
"The number doesn't matter. We Blues are extremely brave," said Armand the Twelfth. Victor the Second replied, "We Reds, of course, are fearless."

AT LUNCHTIME, the Blues and the Reds were still waiting for the Yellows. Waiting can make anyone nervous, even the brave and fearless. "Sir," said Armand the Twelfth, "Since we face eight hundred men, perhaps we should become allies."
"I think we should," agreed Victor the Second.

The allies waited all afternoon.
At dinnertime, they sent out for sandwiches.
They decided to spend all night on the battlefield,
in case the Yellow Army tried to sneak up on them.

ON THE SECOND DAY, the Yellow Army still didn't arrive. The soldiers began to pitch tents and light campfires. On the third day, some of the soldiers' wives came to the battlefield. They brought pots and ladles, for soldiers can't live on sandwiches alone.

On the fourth day, the women brought their babies. And on the fifth day, the other children felt lonely, so they followed their mothers. They brought their cows, pigs, and chickens. The older children began to trade back and forth.

AND ON THE TENTH DAY, the battlefield looked like a village. Fabien thought, "The Reds thought I cheated, and the Blues thought I was useless. I don't have an army, and I never did. But I still ended the war."

FABIEN VISITED Basil the Fourth, the king of the Yellows, to tell him the story. Basil laughed over Fabien's imaginary army, but he cried when he heard Prince Julius was dead. And he cried for the soldiers who had died in the war, even though he didn't know their names.

BASIL THE FOURTH saw that Fabien was clever and brave.
Because the king of the Yellows had no son of his own,
he asked Fabien to become the prince of the Yellows.

Many years later, when Fabien was king, he ruled wisely and long.
And, of course, under King Fabien, no one fought a single war.

First American edition published in 2001 by Carolrhoda Books, Inc.
Translated by Marie-Christine Rouffiac and Tom Streissguth.
Translation copyright © 2001 by Carolrhoda Books, Inc.

Copyright © 1998 by l'école des loisirs, Paris
All rights reserved.
Originally published by l'école des loisirs, under the title *La Guerre*.

Carolrhoda Books, Inc.
A division of Lerner Publishing Group
241 First Avenue North
Minneapolis, MN 55401 U.S.A.

Website address: www.lernerbooks.com

Library of Congress Cataloging-in-Publication Data
Vaugelade, Anais.
[Guerre. English.]
The war / written and illustrated by Anais Vaugelade.—1st American ed.
p. cm.
"Originally published in 1998 by l'école des loisirs, Paris, under the title *La Guerre*."
Summary: Prince Fabien uses an ingenious trick to end the war between the Reds and Blues without violence.
ISBN 1—57505—562—7 (lib. bdg.)
[1. War—Fiction. 2. Princes—Fiction.] I. Title.
PZ7.V448 War 2001
[E]—dc21   009641
1 2 3 4 5 6—JR—06 05 04 03 02 01